The Wind

The Wind

Jay Caselberg

NEWCON
PRESS

NewCon Press
England

First published in the UK by NewCon Press
41 Wheatsheaf Road, Alconbury Weston, Cambs, PE28 4LF
September 2017

NCP 129 (limited edition hardback)
NCP 130 (softback)

10 9 8 7 6 5 4 3 2 1

ISBN:

978-1-910935-53-8 (hardback)
978-1-910935-54-5 (softback)

Cover art by Vincent Sammy
Cover layout by Andy Bigwood

Minor editorial meddling by Ian Whates
Book layout by Storm Constantine

Who has seen the wind? Neither you nor I, but when the trees bow down their heads, the wind is passing by.

– Christina Rossetti

One

A random gust scattered the leaves before him, swirling them up and then letting them tumble and disperse again. Gerry pulled his coat tighter. He could feel the chill even through the thick wool, tugging at his ears through the warm hat he'd put on to help brave the weather. Winter hadn't arrived yet, wouldn't do for a couple of months, but it was cold enough for him to believe that it was upon them already. He bunched his arms around himself and, head down, continued walking down the street. His eyes were watering with the cold and he grimaced. You could smell the cold, not only feel it, and on a day like this, in the depths of autumn, that smell was tinged with something else, the scent of old vegetation, leaf mould and damp, cracked wood. It was there if you opened your senses enough. He'd hate to be out here with nowhere to go, no one to rely on; not that Gerry really had anyone to rely on, apart from himself.

Abbotsford lay close to the woods, so it wasn't unusual, he thought to himself, that he might catch scent of that lush undergrowth as well, borne by the breeze. This was something different though than the smell of summer grasses or of newly mown hay, neither of which were unusual in the high summer months throughout their little rural community. There were tales told about the woods, but nothing he was inclined to take to heart. Every village had its local superstitions, and in that,

Abbotsford was no different from any other smallish community. Oh, they had a post office, a small church, and not one but two locals, as well as a small supermarket and a corner shop, which was where he was headed now. The local bus ran people into the smoke if they wanted to go, regular as clockwork. During the week there were few kids on the streets, as the nearest school was a good seven miles away. Far enough to keep them out of mischief, he supposed. At least daytime mischief, anyway. It had to be said, though, things happened in Abbotsford, probably just pranks, but they happened all the same. It didn't hurt for the locals to foster the legends, whether the kids were responsible or not. Thinking about it, though, he'd never heard them given a name, these things that happened, or whatever was supposed to be responsible for them.

Gerry had moved to Abbotsford about six months ago, freshly out of veterinary college, his first real posting. The old vet had retired and there was enough business to prompt the need for a new one with the surrounding farms, though, really, he would have preferred a local suburban practice: cats, dogs, and canaries rather than wading through pig slop in the teeming rain or being elbow-deep up the back of a cow, the stink of manure and other unmentionables all over him. There would be plenty of opportunity to move on and take the next step, though. He'd gone for what he could get at the time – competition for the city practices was fierce – and, despite the misgivings, he still saw this as an opportunity. The experience afforded by the Abbotsford practice would stand him in good stead, as he saw it. He had no steady relationship and his parents, well, that was another story altogether. Best not to think too much about them, although every time he tried not to they popped straight into his thoughts. It was kind of like that old thing, don't think of an elephant.

Milk and bread; that was what he was down for today. Maybe some bacon. He couldn't think of anything else right at the moment. He preferred the little corner store run by old Mrs Marchant rather than the impersonal service at the so-called supermarket, small though it was, with its gleaming fluorescent tubes and the shiny metallic display cases. If there was any gossip to be had, you'd find it at Marchant's because Ivy had her finger on the pulse of everything that went on in Abbotsford and the surrounding area and shy she was not.

He stood at the corner, checking for traffic, of which there was none, and briefly watched the wind playing with a small trail of leaf litter. Funny how it could look as if small feet were traipsing through, kicking up little plumes of broken leaf and bits of other small detritus, a colourful wrapper or stray scrap of plastic amongst them. He shook his head. Perception was a funny thing. Invisible somethings prancing through the leaves. And there, look, back the other way. An unseen presence was running circles around him in the breeze. Yeah, right. He gave himself a small amused grunt and turned down the High Street, heading towards Marchant's. Small gusts continued to tug at him along the way, almost feeling like tiny invisible fingers pulling random pinches of cloth from his trouser legs, or reaching up to ruffle his hair.

The Marchant's family shop boasted something of everything and probably a few things that you'd never think about. It stood dead on the corner, faded grey-blue paint and old style small-paned windows framed in wood. Nothing like the modern display windows you'd see on shops in town. Gerry wouldn't have been surprised to peer through smeared windows, but Ivy kept the place scrupulously clean. He wondered how long the small establishment had stood here. Probably forever and a day and, as far as he could tell, it had always been a shop. The spring in the overhead door closer creaked as he pushed it open and a small bell tinkled his entry, not that it was needed, because Ivy Marchant was there in her place behind the old style wooden counter and display case, all pale-yellow cardigan, curled hair, and pallid jowly cheeks with a touch of rouge. Her smoke grey eyes looked up and fixed him as he entered. He wouldn't have been a bit surprised if she were sporting fluffy slippers up behind the counter. He could almost imagine her, a fag hanging out of the corner of her mouth, a bundled robe, and curlers under a scarf to go with the slippers, but that was not Ivy. She was always immaculately turned out as far as she probably saw it.

The interior was dim, but there was enough light from the front windows to see everything you needed to. Shelves ran all the way around, except for the small door leading into the rear. A staircase to the upper level probably lay back there, leading up to what must be the living quarters, though a small curtain formed a border, effectively concealing whatever might lie beyond it. No one went back there but Ivy. On a couple of shelves stood old-style big sweet jars with humbugs and other things, although the glass-topped counter had a rack of more modern looking sugary products and chocolates. There were various items stacked on the shelf below the counter's glass surface. He'd never paid much mind as to what might lie there; generally, he just came to stock up his essentials rather than fossicking. He peered down into the case and then did a quick scan of the shelves.

"Ah, Mister Summerfield. Has our local veterinary run out of supplies again?"

Ivy's voice quickly brought him back to the matter at hand.

"Morning, Mrs Marchant. It appears I've done exactly that. I'm going to grab a loaf of bread and some milk, I think. Maybe some bacon."

"Oh, just the thing, weather like this. A nice hot bacon sandwich. Just the job. Lashings of butter. And it's got to be butter. None of that margarine stuff. I don't care what those medicos say. You can't beat proper butter, now can you? Young man like you…"

Gerry nodded and grabbed what he was after, placing them on the counter.

"You'll be wanting some brown sauce with that. You're sure you've got some? Never have too much brown sauce."

"Yes, I think so." He wasn't sure, though, so he stepped over to one of the tall shelves packed with various items, following the direction of Mrs Marchant's lifted chin.

"There we go. Now, Mr. Summerfield. Will that be all? Have you done anything about getting yourself a nice young lady yet? I'm sure there are plenty around who'd be interested in a tall young fellow like yourself. And a veterinary to boot. Nothing wrong with that. Though you could do with a bit more meat on your bones, to my mind."

"So my mother used to tell me, Mrs. Marchant. But no, 'fraid not." Always the inevitable question. He couldn't fathom why Mrs Marchant was so interested in his love life. "There just doesn't seem to be much of an opportunity."

"Now, now. Call me Ivy. Don't know how many times I need to tell you that."

"Yes, well, um, Ivy. There really doesn't seem to be the chance or much of an opportunity hereabouts. Time enough for that, I suppose. And while we're at it, you should be calling me Gerry too. None of this Mr. Summerfield business."

Truth be told, the idea of finding someone of the opposite persuasion was not unattractive, however, what he'd said was true enough; there was not much of a choice in Abbotsford. He'd had a couple of speculative glances in his direction at one of the locals, but well, not his type really, even if he had a type. And, farmer's daughters notwithstanding, the respective farmers were guaranteed to be his clients. Never knew what sort of complications that might lead to.

"Well, you shouldn't leave it too long. Before you know it, the time will have passed you by. Forty-six good years I had with my Alf. Forty-six good years of companionship and succour through the lean times and the fat. We always stood by each other, even through the Dark Days."

Gerry frowned a little at that. He had heard the implied capitalisation in her voice, but he hesitated to ask. He needn't have bothered, though. Ivy was, as ever, ready to seize the opportunity.

"And mark my words," she continued. "The Dark Days will be back. The signs are brewing. It's time. It won't be long now. You never know *when* they are going to come, but come they will. You get yourself fixed up with a nice young lady. She'll keep you safe. When the wind comes through those woods…"

"What's that about the woods?" he asked, curiosity getting the better of his good sense. Once Ivy got started, well…

She leaned forward a little with the next as if taking him into a confidence. "There are things dwell in those woods you don't want to know about," she said, shaking her head. "We abide them here in Abbotsford. That's what we do. And, truth be told, they abide us. And just as well they do. That's what we've done for years. Live and let live I say. Live and let live. But when the wind stirs and stalks across those fields with its long legs, and the things it carries with it… Well, enough about that." She stood back up, pursed her lips, and shook her head.

She fixed him with a stern eye, her lips tight, but the look quickly passed. She seemed to have said her piece. He considered drawing her out further about these 'things in the woods,' but then thought better of it. The last thing he wanted to do was spend the rest of the morning stuck in Marchant's being regaled with the local superstitions. Villagers were villagers, after all, and Ivy was no exception.

"Okay, Ivy. Duly noted," he said. "Just this lot then, for now."

"Right you are then."

He paid and she handed over the change. He took the proffered shopping bag and turned for the door.

"You'll have to pay me for those bags soon," she said. "Not that I hold with it, but that's what we've got to do. Supposed to be doing it already. That's the law. Something to do with the environment. Around here, the environment tends to itself. Still, as I say…"

Gerry merely nodded. "Fair enough. See you soon," he said, pulling open the door and stepping out to the street before she could get properly started again.

"You take good care now," Ivy called after him as the door closed and the small bell tinkled his departure. "And mark my words, do something about finding yourself a young lady, or even a young man."

From Ivy, that last surprised him. Who would have thought? Gerry stood outside the shop for a few moments considering, as the wind tugged at his coat and ruffled the plastic bag in his hand. A sudden gust flapped at the plastic violently, tearing it this way and that. He really should have remembered to wear gloves; the cold was throbbing in his knuckles. Nothing for it. She was right... about the bacon sandwich rather than a young lady. Although... No, a nice hot bacon sandwich sounded like just the thing right now. The stiff breeze tugged at his hair. He'd let it grow out a bit since he'd been in Abbotsford, and maybe it was time to do something about that but, to do so, he'd have to make the journey into town. A hairdresser was the last thing that the village of Abbotsford would boast. He wondered how Ivy managed to maintain her tightly styled curls. She was always in place behind that counter, and he couldn't remember ever having seen her anywhere else. Perhaps there was a travelling hairdresser or some such. Maybe a woman who did home visits.

The place he was renting was a low bungalow style small residence with a grey slate roof and chimney. Somebody had said that it was an old chapel that had been converted. Of course, with the local church, he didn't understand why Abbotsford would also need a chapel, so maybe that was just a story. There was hardly the population to support multiple places of worship. Be that as it may, the place was pleasant enough, and the fireplace would make things cosy during the long winter darkness, although he'd not yet had a chance to try it out. And, thinking about it, there had been no evidence of a wood supply, although the fireplace had clearly been used and he assumed it was functional. He'd have to do something about that as well. Perhaps he could make a trip at the weekend to the sacred Abbotsford wood and do a bit of foraging, though it was probably just as easy to find some sort of local firewood supplier. He could look into the matter later, but really, the excuse for an excursion was just as good. He'd seen a lot of the surrounding area on his callouts and doing his rounds, but always barns and fields and stables, not yet the woods themselves. Of course, he'd have to check the chimney as well. He hadn't even taken the trouble to look up inside it since he'd moved in.

The house, which he'd sort of inherited from the old vet, also had a rear room that had been converted into a functional little surgery but, till now, Gerry had only needed to use it the once for one of the local pets. The bulk of his work was out in the field. This had its advantages, but with the season closing in, he wasn't really looking forward to the mud and the rime. His first winter in Abbotsford was fast approaching and he had no real idea what it was likely to bring. If he'd taken Ivy's words to heart, it could be more than just wind, rain, and snow. In fact, the things she had said were starting to make him a little uneasy. What on Earth were these 'Dark Days' she had mentioned? No, he shook the thoughts away. Just idle village superstition. That was all.

There was nothing in his agenda for the afternoon, and he took his time readying breakfast: greasy, full of cholesterol and dripping with rich, melted butter and layers of bacon. Just what was needed to fend off the approach of his impending cold. Just as Ivy, in her infinite wisdom had recommended. Wiping melted grease from the slick dripping from his chin, Gerry felt somewhat more fortified against the rest of the morning and even more, what the coming afternoon might offer. Later, well after lunch, he needed to drive out to one of the distant farms, more as a courtesy call rather than to deal with anything wrong, He had no particular love for cattle, but they were part of his regular responsibility these days. Stupid animals, all in all. Not as stupid as sheep, but stupid all the same. Not like horses. As things stood, he had plenty of time before he had to get into his old Vauxhall Combo and wind his way along through the narrow winding roads to get to the farm in question, passing along the hedge-lined streets or between rough stone walls which hid the open fields from view. He'd decided on the van when he'd first arrived in Abbotsford, buying it in town at a used-car dealership. Though the van had seen better days, it was practical enough to serve his needs and the price had been right. It would do the job until he was ready to move on, for he wasn't likely to stay in Abbotsford for ever. Just like his practice, the van was an interim thing, just like his life here. Not that he really had any plans about what he might do after Abbotsford. He had time yet to work all that out. The village, the farms, the local practice, they were just a stepping stone. There wasn't anything here to hold him forever. One day, he supposed he'd devote some time to considering what this current situation might be a stepping stone towards. But that was typical. As his teachers used to say: bright enough, but no real ambition. Gerry Summerfield, destined for mediocre things…

Having cleaned up breakfast and consumed enough coffee to get him through the morning, Gerry considered researching this whole local wood collection business, but then had second thoughts. Regardless of any regulations, he was sure that nobody would begrudge him a little firewood scavenging. In fact, thinking about it, he rather doubted there would to be anyone to see. There was the wood, and there was the village, and the farms, and that was about it. Not that he really knew about such things, but it was probably hunting season already. He had, as yet, not seen any hunters since he'd arrived in the area. He knew that a couple of miles away there was a manor house where the owners, whoever they were, raised racehorses, but he had not had any cause to visit, as they employed their own resident vet. Nice enough for some. If there *was* hunting, then they were likely to be the type, all tweed, and Range Rovers; unless, of course, there were local poachers, but he hadn't seen anyone like that either.

No, a visit to the wood was definitely in order, and if there were any real regulation about collecting firewood, he could simply claim ignorance. With a slight pang of conscience, he did a bit of online research at the kitchen table, but was soon overwhelmed by the depth and breadth of information and the pages and pages of regulations, most of them set in historical precedent. With a snort and a shake of his head, he flipped the laptop shut. A town like Abbotsford, there was bound to be something buried in history that related to such things. No, claiming ignorance was definitely the best bet, though what was that argument he'd heard quoted on cop shows? Ignorance was no defence?

Leaving his mug and plate to drain beside the sink, he grabbed his coat and headed out to the van. There was enough room in the back to load anything he might gather for a while, at least. He stood at the front door, feeling the cold breeze tugging wilfully at his clothes. The sky was cloudy, but it didn't feel like rain. A slight gust riffled the grass nearby, a sound, a whisper. He cocked his head, listening, and then frowned. No, it was nothing more than his imagination working overtime. He shook his head and reaching into his pocket for his keys, made his way over to the van. Reaching for the door, he fumbled the keys, dropped them into the grass. Somewhere off behind them, he almost thought he heard a chuckle. Clearing his throat, his mouth set in a firm line, Gerry reached again for the keys and shook his head. He really did need to get out and about. Too much time on his own seemed to be playing with his imagination. Now he was starting to hear things. Perhaps Ivy's suggestions wasn't too far off the mark after all.

As he snagged the keys and reached once more for the car door, he took a quick look around, but there was no one there, no one to blame for the sounds, just the breeze eddying and teasing at the long grass and wild unkempt bushes bordering the small yard behind his cottage. He watched as a brown and drying leaf rocked back and forth on the old wooden table. Now where had that come from? There were no trees hereabouts. He watched it for a moment more, and then gave a slight shrug. Taking one last look around, he climbed into the van and shut the breeze away with the solid clunk of his car door.

"Right," he said to himself and kicked the engine into life. It coughed once and then caught, and he looked back over his shoulder as he backed out onto the street.

Two

"Tom," said Ivy, not moving, keeping her gaze fixed on the window, not meeting his eyes.

"Ivy," he said in reply. He didn't bother making eye contact either, just let his gaze rove around the dimness of the shop, at the shelves. He waited for the door to close and then looked down at his boots, green, black, and muddy. He said nothing for a few moments, merely stood there. Finally, he cleared his throat and spoke.

"So, what do you think?" he said, without lifting his gaze.

Ivy, her mouth set in a tight line, gave her head a little shake. "I don't know. It might be. It might not be. Everything's telling me it is."

"Well, we need to make a decision soon. He is the veterinary after all."

"Yes, I know that," she snapped. "Don't you think I know that? If it is, then what other choice do we have? Tell me that. But I don't want you to go around saying anything to the others yet. Is that clear?"

Tom gave a deep sigh. "Well it's going to be soon. All the signs are there, aren't they? And when the signs are there, you know what happens. She'll be back."

"And I know that too, Thomas Mills."

Finally, she turned her face to look at him, her eyes narrowed.

Tom merely rubbed at his chin, grimaced and then turned to the door. As he reached for the handle he gave another sigh and turned back. "I need some flour."

"Right then," said Ivy. She turned away and reached behind her to one of the shelves, stretching up to snag one of the packages neatly arrayed up there. Slowly she turned and placed it on the glass countertop before her. "That'll be one eighty, Tom."

"Right," he said, fumbled in his pockets for the coins and clicked them down on the counter. "That's all," he said, grabbed the packet, and turned away.

As he pulled the door open and the bell tinkled once more, she called after him.

"We'll know soon enough," she said.

"It'd be a pity, is all," muttered Tom as he stepped out into the street and wandered off, his head bowed, packet of flour clutched before him, his cap pulled down firmly on his head, his thick ratty coat hunched on his shoulders, not bothering to spare a backward glance.

Ivy stared at the road where he had been for several minutes after he'd gone.

Abbotsford lay in a low valley, surrounded by hills, mostly devoted to pastureland, but to the west lay the wood, a clear wall of vegetation marking its start. On the slope leading down from the front edge, the fields lay mostly ungrazed, a few white and grey stones protruding from the lumpy ground. As Gerry wound his way along the unsealed path leading up, he took all this in. Much of the wood was still green, though there were clear patches of brown and orange scattered throughout. He chewed his lip as he negotiated the narrow, rutted track in the van. Ivy's words had struck home for some reason, and they niggled at him now. It was nothing that she'd said directly, but they'd set him to thinking. Considering his life, everything he'd done up till now, none of it was really purposeful; there was never any tangible end goal in mind.

It was her talk of finding a nice young woman that had set him off. Relationships were no different, not that he'd ever been much of a lady's man. He'd had a couple of longer-term associations, though there had never been any real sense of permanence about them. It was as if they'd merely been marking time together. There'd been Janette at school, but that had been the start of his first real, awkward, fumbling explorations, and then there'd been Caroline in college. That had lasted a full two years. Somehow, though, it was commitment without real dedication, both of them filling in the space, going through the motions. Caroline had been big, blonde, and horsey and had taken the lead, Gerry quite content to just follow along. He'd been aware, somehow, right from the start, that he wasn't meant to be the one. Caroline needed someone more solid, perhaps someone from the hunting, shooting and fishing set. That, Gerry was not. Really, they must have looked a pair, him with his long, gangly, weedy frame and she like a girls' school sports mistress. He'd been content enough to go with the flow while the relationship ran its course, as inevitably it did, but perhaps that had been the problem. It was just too easy to go with the flow. Oh, he was bright enough, he supposed, but he had yet to find anything that truly inspired him. His mother had desperately wanted him to go into medicine, but that too was part of the problem. He'd not quite made the cut. Veterinary Science had been the next best thing, and for once in his life he'd had to apply himself to manage that. Maybe if he'd applied himself to a few more things in life, he'd be better off. Applying himself to a relationship might have been a start. He'd always imagined himself ending up with a wife, a couple of kids, a nice house in the suburbs or in the city somewhere, but right now it seemed he was a long way away from that. He wondered if true love was a thing that came naturally or something that you had to work at. He'd never seemed to be able to find it.

The track ended at a moss-covered wooden gate, closed, but lying slightly askew on its posts. Gerry stopped and got out, walked over to the gate, and shook it tentatively. He scanned the empty field beyond, scattered with hummocks, weeds, nettles, and the occasional outcropping of stones. The field was devoid of any defined tracks and the wall of vegetation formed an unbroken line on the other side. But then he spotted a slight gap over to one side that could be the start of a path. He scanned the surrounding land, but there was not a person in sight. A few cows stood grazing further back down the hill, but that was it. He debated with himself for a couple of moments, but then made up his mind. There was clearly no one around, and although there seemed to be no evidence of vehicles having crossed the rough field over to the wood, he was better off bringing the car over to the edge rather than having to lug lumps of wood back across the field to load into the van, assuming he actually managed to gather any.

Lifting the gate at one end to drag it open took a bit more effort than anticipated. The wood was damp, mossy and felt almost soft beneath his hands. With a sigh, he realised that he should have thought to bring some gloves. Still, too late now. Having attended to the gate, he got back in the van and eased it through, stopped, leaving the motor running and got out to return and pull the gate shut again. One thing you learned very quickly out in the country: livestock or not, you didn't leave gates open. He got back into the van, and very slowly negotiated his way across the field, weaving around a couple of uneven patches towards the gap in the growth, parked beside the trees and killed the engine. He sat there for a few moments, not moving, just looking. He could tell that the wood was old, ancient even. Small shrubs and some spindly trees grew along the edges, already brown and orange leaf litter covering the ground around their bases, but further in, through the undergrowth, he could see other, more massive trunks and branches. He knew very little about trees, could perhaps name a few of the more common varieties. He recognised yew, oak, a couple of others, but the rest were mainly just trees. Some of these, though, were clearly very, very old. Distorted wooden faces peered out at him through the undergrowth and strangely twisted branches wound grotesquely above the ground below. Long sinuous roots crawled across the ground here and there, humped and knobbly, pale and wrinkled, like unnaturally long, jointed fingers. A breeze ruffled the remaining leaves and the spindly branches along the edges like a breath. Taking a deep breath of his own, he opened the door and stepped out of the van.

The gap between the trees appeared to be natural rather than man made, almost an archway, branches leaning over to clasp hands above the wanderer passing below. Small hillocks and depressions stretched out between the trunks, all carpeted in fallen leaves and twigs, browns, oranges, and yellows. Here and there a puff of wind stirred them, or whipped them into spirals. He stood there beneath the branches and, for some unknown reason, felt a chill. It wasn't the cold. It was just… something else. Nor was it particularly dark here. Grey, misty light filtered down through the branches from the pewter sky. Further in it seemed to grow gloomier, but for the moment, he had no real intention of venturing into the heart of the wood. All around him was the smell of vegetation, earth, slowly decaying leaves, and old, old wood. He scanned the surrounding ground, crouching down to get a better perspective, but all he could see were a few fallen twigs. Here, at least, there was nothing sizeable. Knowing his luck, some enterprising soul had likely been here before him and cleaned everything out. He let out a deep sigh and stood back up. It seemed he'd have to go further in after all. He looked at the roughly defined pathway but decided that sadly there was no real way he could get the van in here. Around him, branches moved against branches making an odd scraping sound that drifted around the thick and twisted trunks. All about came the susurrus of leaves shifting in the wind almost suggesting whispered voices of children. He stopped and listened to the sounds and then realised something else. He would have expected to hear bird noise, see evidence of local wildlife, but there was nothing, nothing other than the murmuring of the trees. It was almost as if the wood sucked away all sound from outside. There wasn't even the drone of a distant plane. He humphed to himself and, brushing his hands one against the other, headed further into the depths. *Curiouser and curiouser*, he thought as little by little the light faded around him.

Three

Ivy had never expected herself to be married off at the tender age of nineteen, but it was not so uncommon in that day and age. It was more the manner of its coming to pass that was unusual. Back then, they had not had the store. That was solely under the proprietorship of the Marchant family. George, the old man, would open in the early hours and then stay open till late. The family didn't live above the shop, as Ivy did today, but had a cottage on the outskirts of the village, nothing fancy, but adequate for the George, Susanne, and their son, Alfred. Ivy had barely known the boy. He was a good eight years older than her. Of course, she knew him enough to nod in passing, but that was about the extent of it. Ivy's father was a simple pig farmer, her mother, well, she kept house. She did more than keep house, though, and she instilled her growing daughter with the local lore. It was probably this, and the events that took place in the ensuing years, that led to her and Alf never having children of their own. Despite that, she never regretted their decision and she had no regrets about their life. Far better to be a shopkeeper than a pig farmer. She still remembered that smell. Some days, when the wind was right, she could almost taste it on the breeze.

One morning, her mother called her in and sat her down at the kitchen table.

"Ivy," she said. "We need to have a talk."

All wide-eyed and unsuspecting, she had taken her place at the table, wondering what she had done this time.

"Now I want you to listen to me. Don't react. Don't ask questions. There'll be time enough for that later. Right now, just listen."

"But what is it —?"

"Hsss," her mother stilled her with a raised finger. "Just listen now."

Ivy bit her lip and sat, quiet, waiting.

"I've tried to tell you everything I know. Everything that you need to know. You know about the Dark Days. You know about what the wind can bring. Your grandmother used to tell you the tales. You know what to look for. You've seen them for yourself, or at least you've seen the signs. They *are* back again, or at least they are coming back. You must have noticed them."

Ivy nodded, slowly.

"Well, it seems she's coming back too. It's been a long time, but I can see the signs. The wind-borne things are worse than last time, and the time before that. Much worse. I can feel it. Others can see too. The way this is building, it can only mean one thing."

Ivy said nothing.

"The Lady of the Wood is coming back."

"But what does that —?"

"Ssss! I told you no questions. Just listen. She is the one. And you know what they say. If your heart does not belong to another, it belongs to her. We've lost too many good young men from this town over the ages. The choice is simple. Keep them safe or they are hers, now and forever. And so has it always been."

Ivy frowned, then. Her mother nodded slowly.

"I want you to do something. You might not like what I'm going to tell you, but it is what we have to do. The Marchants are good people. Their boy, Alf, is a good boy. They can't afford to lose him. They need him. You have to understand that. And here in Abbotsford we look after our own, so we do. If your grandmother were still here, she'd be telling you the same thing. Your grandmother knew so much more than I do."

Her mother looked thoughtfully out the kitchen window, playing with a towel between her fingers. She just sat there, her smoke grey eyes staring out across the fields into nothingness. After a few moments, she seemed to remember where she was and brought her gaze back into the kitchen and across to her daughter.

"Still," she said. "I wouldn't ask this of you if it wasn't necessary. I've spoken to your father and he knows, so don't think that he doesn't. He agrees with me."

"What?" said Ivy finally. "What is it?"

"You're going to have to marry Alf Marchant."

"What?"

"We've made all of the arrangements," said her mother. "The ceremony will take place on Saturday."

"That's the day after tomorrow!"

"We couldn't arrange it any sooner."

"But wait. This is ridiculous. I can't marry Alf Marchant. I hardly know him. And don't I get a choice in the matter?"

"I'm afraid not, my girl. It's already decided."

Ivy pushed her chair back, the legs protesting against the stone floor, stood, leaned across the table. "I will not!"

"I'm going to call your father now," her mother told her.

There had been more arguments, tears, protests, but in the end it was as her mother had told her. That Saturday, nearly forty-nine years ago to the day, Ivy Wilson had married Alfred Marchant at a simple ceremony in the local church. There were a few villagers there. Every single one of them had appeared to know exactly what was going on. They had smiled and nodded, and shook their hands, as if it were the most natural thing in the world. It had all seemed, to Ivy, like some sort of bizarre dream that she was caught in.

But that had been then. Ivy didn't regret any of it. Not for a moment.

As he pushed deeper into the wood, the light grew steadily gloomier, the trees larger, older, more twisted. Here and there stood hollow trunks and broader trees, obviously gone, but still with branches. Gerry would have thought with so much dead vegetation there'd be plenty of fallen branches or logs lying around, but there was nothing. Leaf litter covered the ground, but even the twigs were sparse. Eventually he reached a clearing, only it wasn't really a clearing. A large ancient tree dominated the centre of the space, the wood deep red. It almost looked as if multiple trunks had been joined together and there was a hollow in between them like an arched doorway, or a church door. The clustered trunks resembled a collection of priests standing on either side, guarding the entranceway. Spiralling and twisting out from the trunk stretched thick, knotted branches. Green needle leaves sprung in profusion from the twigs. He crouched down on his haunches and peered into the blackness of the hollow. Above him air moved, causing the branches to creak, rustling the needles. The ground seemed bare, not even tracks of animals, certainly not footprints. He knew, intuitively, that this was a yew, but it was unlike any he had ever seen. It must be truly ancient, but how old? He stayed there, just listening, letting his gaze wander over the twisting limbs, smelling the wood and the earth and something else, though he couldn't quite put his finger on what that might be. Fox? No, something else. Definitely organic, but not like any animal spoor he was familiar with. And he a vet. Though wild animals weren't really his forte. He didn't think it was vegetative. The wind stirred and whistled through the wood. A sudden gust from out of nowhere pushed him forward, almost making him lose his balance. He quickly got to his feet. Again, another push from behind as if urging him forward towards that dark hollow at the tree's centre.

Well, as interesting as this was, it was pretty much a loss as far as the stated purpose. No firewood to be found. He supposed he'd have to track down some local supplier after all. He turned away from the tree, trying to remember which way he had come. It should be fairly straightforward. Everything seemed strangely unfamiliar though, darker now. The breeze was steady, pushing from all sides, seeming to come from all directions at once.

"Come on, Gerry, get it together," he said to himself and picked a direction.

From behind him came a sound, like an exhalation of breath, like a sigh.

He stopped in his tracks, turned around.

"Hello? Is there anyone there?"

He scanned the surrounding trees and shadows. It had distinctly sounded like someone's voice.

"Hello?"

Nothing. Merely the sound of the wind and the branches.

He turned again, seeking his way.

From off to the left came another noise, almost like a chuckle. He was imagining it, had to be; nothing more than branches moving one against the other in the wind. That could produce a sound like that, couldn't it? Like a cricket's legs.

He swallowed and stepped forward again and then another step after that. In the next few moments, the wind picked up and then the first few large drops spattered down through the branches above.

When, at last, he struggled back to the van, he was soaked through. So much for that little adventure. Good idea, Summerfield.

Right, nothing for it but to get back home, get out of these wet things, have a hot shower, and get ready for his scheduled rounds. With the way the rain was coming down, he'd have to be careful heading back across the field. He didn't want to end up getting stuck in the mud. He almost laughed at that. Stuck in the mud, not that he was exactly. No more big ideas for the time being, though. Probably not even medium-sized ones.

The time was approaching. Ivy had seen the signs. No doubt about it; the Quick Ones were back. Those little flashes at the corner of her eyes. Those mysterious little tugs at her clothing. The blurred something in the shadow that was there and yet wasn't there. The voices that were not voices. She knew what to look for. Her grandmother had taught her well, just as she had, in turn, been instructed by her mother, and her mother's mother before that. The last time they had returned, Ivy had been in her prime, and the time before that, she'd been a mere girl. Nobody could tell her what made them choose a particular year, but all the stories agreed on one thing: this was the season they appeared. She looked out onto the street, watched a stray scrap of paper blowing down its length. There was nothing for it. She needed to go and talk to some people. If she didn't do it soon, they'd be coming to see her. If they didn't start doing something s, matters would be taken out of their hands. She'd never actually seen it happen herself, but she'd heard the tales, as they all had. Old Albert had seen it, but he was gone now. Had been these couple of years. A pity really. With her lips tightly pressed together, Ivy shook her head, stepped around from behind the counter, crossed to the door and turned the sign to announce that she was closed. Even seeing that would be enough to alert a few of the locals that something was going on. With a sigh, she turned back to the rear of the shop and ducked past the curtain to head upstairs and prepare herself. There were people to talk to, things to arrange. They'd need to be ready. They always had to be ready for the Lady of the Wood or there'd be regret. Regret and sorrow. That much was assured.

By the time Gerry had got himself cleaned up and changed, ready to head out, the sky had cleared up. The dark clouds had made way for patchy breaks of blue, though the light would fade soon, so he'd better get on his way.

Alfred Wickford's farm lay on the other side of the wood and Gerry had to drive a circuitous route to get there through narrow and winding laneways. He wondered how some of these people managed to get their farm machinery along these restrictive byways. He hoped he wasn't about to meet something coming the other way and be forced to back all the way to the last intersection. He reached his destination without incident, however, made his way up to the small stone cottage and the large barn. Alf had clearly heard him coming, and was out in front waiting as he pulled the van to a halt. He stepped out, retrieved his bag from the back and walked out to greet the grizzled old farmer.

"She's in the barn," said Alf, without any pause for niceties.

"Right then." "She's off her feed, looking poorly."

Gerry pursed his lips and nodded in response. "I'd better see to her then," he said.

"Right you are. Let me know when you're done."

And that was that. Alf turned and made his way back to the cottage.

Finding his own way into the barn, Gerry soon determined that there was nothing obviously serious ailing the cow, gave her a shot just to stave off anything, and packed his gear away again. He washed up in an old stone sink after stripping off his gloves and rinsing them off. He could hear the wind thrumming in gusts against the old roof, and then all was quiet. Giving one last glance at the cow, who returned his gaze with a walleyed stare, he shrugged, and hefted his bag, ready to be on his way. He supposed he'd better bear the glad tidings to Alf back at the cottage. As he stepped out of the barn, he saw someone leaning on the fence across the yard in the direction of the woods watching him. Did Alf have a daughter? He didn't think so. Well, not as far as he knew. He could be wrong, though. He wandered over to the back of the van, stowed his bag and then strolled over in the direction of the fence.

"Hello," he said as he grew closer.

Nearer, he could see she had pale, slightly freckled skin, a mass of curling deep red hair and the greenest eyes he'd ever seen. She had on a deep green dress that offset her eyes and hair both at the same time.

"Well, hello," he said again, immediately feeling stupid for having done so.

"Hello to you," she said, a hint of amusement on her lips.

"I'm Gerry, the local vet," he said.

"Yes, I can see that."

"Of course you can." At that moment the wind stirred, floating tresses of that thick red hair up and around her face. She continued watching his eyes, saying nothing.

"And you?" he asked, finally.

"Amanda," she said. "I am Amanda. They say it means 'having to be loved'." She laughed then, deep, and rich as if it were a great joke. She stepped back from the fence, never breaking eye contact.

"Well, Amanda," he said. "It's nice to meet you."

She said nothing in response.

"Um, I guess I should get back to Alf."

She was just on the verge of turning away, when she stopped, turned back.

"I saw you," she said.

"I'm sorry," said Gerry with a slight frown.

"I saw you. In the wood. You were there."

"Um yes, I was. But…"

She smiled and nodded, turned away and started walking off across the field.

"Hey wait…"

She didn't even acknowledge him, merely kept walking unhurriedly away in the direction of that wood. He glanced back over his shoulder in the direction of the cottage. When he looked back, she was gone.

He turned around and wandered up to the cottage, knocked on the door and waited for Alf to appear again.

"She's fine, Alf. I've given her a shot to perk her up. Just keep an eye on her over the next couple of days."

Alf pressed his lips together and gave a nod in understanding.

"Funniest thing just happened," said Gerry. "Do you know a young woman, red hair, goes by the name of Amanda? Well that's what she said her name was."

Alf narrowed his eyes suspiciously. "Why would you ask that?"

"Well I just saw her and –"

"You couldn't have," he said, cutting him off. "Not here." He shook his head. "Not here."

"But…"

"I'm sorry, veterinary. I have to go now." Without another word, he stepped back inside and closed the door, leaving Gerry standing there open-mouthed staring at a sheet of blank and peeling wood.

Gerry finally closed his mouth, thought about knocking again, but then simply shook his head and walked back to his van. Village folk certainly had their peculiarities. Alf Wickford was a rum sort as it was, but this… better not to push it. As he started the van and headed on down the hill, he couldn't help seeing the girl, more rightly young woman, walking confidently away across the fields. She was certainly something, but then there was something strange there too. And then there was Alf's reaction. It was all a little peculiar. Was everyone in this village peculiar? All the way down the hill he was chewing his lip, thinking about it. Perhaps he should find Ivy, ask her about this Amanda. If anyone was likely to know something about her it would be Ivy

Marchant. What was Abbotsford doing with a strangely attractive young woman wandering around the fields? Ivy would be bound to know. No doubt she'd warn him off as well.

Four

They were still living in his parent's old place. Her mother had passed just the previous year. Looking back, Ivy was only a kid really, twenty-four years old and all the weight of the world upon her shoulders, or so it seemed at the time. Since that first Saturday a few years previously, she had grown fond of Alf, though she couldn't say properly whether she really loved him. That would come in time, or so she hoped. She was used to having him around at least, and he wasn't too demanding as you might expect a husband to be. His parents were getting on a bit too, as was her own father. He still worked the old farm, and she tried to get out to see him as much as she could, but now that Alf's parents were less mobile she spent a lot of time working in the shop, helping out, as did Alf. In the times that she did manage to get out to the farm, her father was as surly as ever. Spending so much time with only himself for company didn't seem to help matters. She had to admit, she secretly dreaded those visits. Not only was he a gruff old man with barely a word to say, but the smell never went away either.

Once or twice there'd been the inevitable and not so subtle hints from the elder Marchants about the possibility of another generation, but ultimately Ivy deflected them however she could. She wasn't quite ready for that yet.

And then things started breaking.

This year it was early, in the first couple of weeks of September. The wind had started picking up in earnest and the signs were all around her. It looked as if it was going to be a bad one. Despite all the teaching, the things that had been drilled into her, Ivy missed her mother, her grandmother. Where were they to give her confirmation when she lacked the confidence in herself? She first noticed the tugging at her dress on her morning walk to the shop. She knew she couldn't see them, knew they'd remain hidden, only teasing at the edges of her vision, or playing little tricks with pieces of paper or leaves along her way. If they were here, though, it could only mean one thing. Her mother and grandmother had told her there was only one solution; the Lady had to be appeased. You didn't want to think about the consequences if she wasn't. Ivy shook her head as she stood there behind the counter staring out at the street and watching the wind tugging at people's coats and scarves. And there was Chris Oldthwaite charging down the road after his hat as it tumbled end over end away from his grasp. Lord knows, she'd thought about moving, getting right out of Abbotsford and away, but where would she go? Where would any of them go? Her grandmother used to tell her that once you were a part of Abbotsford, then you were a part of it. Something would always conspire to make sure that you stayed.

She heard Alf stirring upstairs and the creak of his shoes upon the staircase. A moment later, he ducked out from the back room and took up position beside her.

"Feel like a break?" he asked. "Maybe go upstairs, have a nice cup of tea and a bit of a sit down? I'll take over here for a while. It seems pretty quiet."

"It's the weather. Not too many people want to be out and about in this wind."

"There is that."

"It's not only the wind, Alf. You know that."

He didn't say anything in response, merely plucked at his lower lip.

"Listen, Alf. I know you don't like talking about it, but they're here. The Quick Ones are back again."

He slowly lowered his hand to the counter, pressed his lips together and let out a long breath of air through his nose, almost a sigh, but not quite. Something else.

"You talk to me, Alf Marchant. This is no time for one of your silences."

"What do you want me to say, Ivy? You know more than I do. What am I supposed to tell you? What am *I* supposed to do about it?" He turned to face her then, a pleading look on his face.

"I know, I know. It's beyond all of us. But we have to do something."

"What?"

"Something…"

They both turned back to look out at the street again.

"I only wish I knew what," said Ivy, her voice barely audible.

Alfred lifted one arm, put it around her back and gently rested one hand upon her shoulder.

Perhaps it was because her mother had never been much of a reader, or a writer if it came to that. She didn't even write shopping lists, just carried everything around in her head. The problem was, there was just so much you could carry. By the time Ivy and Alf got married, she was starting to forget things. There was no way of knowing how much she had forgotten or simply failed to remember in the time before that. Her grandmother was long gone.

That first bad year when it finally escalated, after all the signs had been growing, they lost Alf's mother. His father took a tumble and ended up in a wheelchair, and by then he was at the point of frailness where he required constant care. A third of the town's livestock fell prey to some mysterious virus, and those raising crops fared little better. Things broke, or simply failed to work. There were intermittent power shortages and on top of that, the milk went bad. Deliveries failed to turn up. Things just seemed to go from bad to worse. Right near Christmas, they lost Ivy's father. He hadn't been ill. One day he simply fell over on the farm and died. After everything had been attended to, they decided there was little for it but to sell the farm and the remaining stock. She didn't hold out much hope of finding a buyer, not with the way things were. In readiness, they started to clear the place out, find whatever they could sell, burn, or donate the rest. It was during that operation that Ivy, fortunately, stumbled across her grandmother's notebooks. Where her mother had lacked the will to put pen to paper, Ivy's grandmother, bless her heart, had been quite the opposite. Notebook after notebook were filled with crabbed and faded writing and sketches, some of it almost illegible, but meticulous in its recording. The ink was strangely brown, the pages yellowing, some of them brittle, but, despite that, most of them were intact enough to decipher. Her grandmother's notebooks were full of everything she had learned, everything she knew and everything that had been passed down to her by her mother and her mother's mother before that.

At first, Ivy didn't realise what she had, but thankfully she thought to keep them. She nearly tossed them with a bunch of other old papers that had been lying in cartons in the old storage room out the back. It was a wonder that the mice and rats hadn't got to them. She took them back to the house and promptly forgot all about them, more concerned about what to do with the farm. As it was, they had to hire a man to look after the animals, an expense they could ill afford. The shop was not doing very well. Nothing in Abbotsford was doing very well. Everyone was scraping their pennies together trying to make ends meet. If only she had discovered what was between those pages earlier, she might have been able to help avoid some of what occurred during those dark months. They had met the Dark Days in their full force, that was for sure.

It was over a month later. The day had been tough and Ivy was looking for something to distract herself. The television was on the blink again and she didn't feel much like listening to the radio. She remembered the box, up in the attic, and went up to dig it out. For the next few hours she sat there, reading, wincing a little as she turned the fragile pages, but with every new piece she read, grasping more and more of what they had been missing. What was happening here went way back, back before any of them remembered. This was more than generations. Abbotsford was an old, old place. She sort of knew that, but it was only her grandmother's writings that brought home to her exactly how old. Within those pages, she learned about the practices and the rites, traditions that had existed for centuries, traditions that would keep the Dark Days at bay, or at least mollify what caused them. She learned that too, and she learned what lived deep within the wind that surrounded them even now.

If only she had realised.

She looked up from the page, her palm flat against the book, and looked out the window at the darkened sky and the darker patch sitting hunched and waiting atop the hill beneath it. The Lady's Wood. It had been there for a long, long time. Longer than any of them. It would probably be there long after they had gone.

Gerry awoke in darkness. He'd been dreaming. He was certain, but what he was not so sure of was what had woken him. His face was slick with sweat, and he felt hot, uncomfortable. His heart was pounding in his ears. The wind whipped around the walls of the cottage and rushed across the roof. He could hear a tapping at one of the windows. Was it tapping? There were no trees around the cottage, no branches to blow against the glass. Untidily, he threw the covers back and stumbled to his feet. He needed a drink of water at least. His mouth felt as if a desert sandstorm had set up home inside. He worked his tongue and lips, trying to find some moisture. The sound of his pulse still beat in his ears, steady, almost in synchronisation with the strange tapping sound and it ran up through the back of his head, like something clenched there. First things first. Get some water from the fridge and then work out what was making that noise. He padded out to the kitchen in his underwear, and it was only by the time he reached the slate floor that he realised he was cold, the sweat cooling on his bare skin. He grabbed the bottle from the fridge and greedily guzzled several swallows. It did a little something to alleviate the dryness in his mouth, but, if anything, only made him feel colder. It did absolutely nothing to relieve the beating pulse in his ears.

He placed the bottle back in the fridge and stood there in the darkness listening, torn between going back and snagging a robe and working out what the heck was making that noise. All the while, snatches of dream images kept swimming up inside his head. There'd been trees, the wood. It had definitely been the wood. He shook his head, trying to get rid of them, but that did little to help the constricted feeling inside his skull. More cautiously, he tilted his head first one way, then the other, trying to get a better bearing on the tapping. It seemed to be coming from the other side of the living room. He headed towards the doorway and stood there. Yes, it was coming from one of the windows. Cautious that he didn't trip over a random piece of furniture in the darkness – it was pitch black outside, completely overcast – he walked carefully over to the other side and peered closer at the window. It wasn't tapping at all. The glass panel was rattling in its frame, vibrating with the pressure of the air buffeting against it. Great. If that was going to go on all night, he wasn't going to get any more sleep. He let out a deep sigh and stood staring, wondering what to do. He needed putty or sealant, and he was pretty sure that he had none. He leaned down to get a better look at the offending seal. Of course he should go back over and switch the light on, but he was here now. He could see the gap where the seal had fallen away or simply dried up, allowing the pane movement in the frame. Perhaps he could find something in the surgery to stick into the gap, hold the glass in place and limit the movement. Maybe one of his scalpels would do the job. Failing that, he could make use of some forceps. He was just deciding, when the glass rattled again, causing him to look up through the window. There, pale, like a fogged impression you got when you breathed on glass, right in the middle of the pane, was what looked like a hand print. But on closer inspection it looked more like some sort of animal track. It was too small for a hand, had three pointed things that could be fingers, and, splayed out from the centre, at the side, was what could pass for a thumb. This also came to a point. No way *that* could be a thumb. He had only seen it because he'd been standing there in darkness. If he'd turned the light on, the reflection from the room would have prevented him from seeing it at all. He crouched down on his haunches and looked more closely. It was definitely on the other side of the glass.

"Huh, strange," he murmured, and stood again.

There was sure to be some logical explanation. A wet leaf could have blown against the glass. That was probably it. Although this certainly didn't look like a leaf. Not really. One of nature's unsolved mysteries.

With that last thought, the glass rattled again, giving him a start and setting his pulse racing once more. He hissed a breath out between tongue and teeth. This bloody weather was starting to drive him a little crazy. What had Ivy Marchant said about things carried in the wind, or something like that? If he didn't watch out he'd be starting to believe this village nonsense soon. Before long he'd be a true Abbotsford local.

Shaking his head, he made for the bedroom to grab a robe, turning on the lights as he went. On the way through, he glanced at the illuminated oven clock. 3:00 a.m. Wasn't that supposed to be the darkest hour?

He ended up finding two pairs of tweezers and pushing them down at either end of the gap, before standing back, waiting, testing out his handiwork. The wind was still making its presence felt, but although he could see the air pushing against the pane, rattling appeared to have gone away for now. Gerry gave a satisfied nod. That would have been that, except for a strange niggling feeling that crept up inside him. Something about the dream, though already it was starting to slip away, had made him uneasy, as dreams often will, but there was something else. He crossed back over to the other side of the room and killed the lights. The living room had windows on two sides, and he just wanted to check. He moved to each of the windows in turn, crouching down and looking at the glass. More looking at the outside of the glass. The first was clear, but the second bore another of those strange prints. He frowned at that, but it could be explained away easily enough. When he got to the fourth one, though, he stopped dead still where he was. On the outside of the glass was not one, but two of those strange prints, and they were either side of another shape, a shape, that could easily be interpreted as a face. He could trace a brow line, what would have been spaces for eyes, two strangely flared nostrils and a puckered, misshapen mouth. It was at the right height for someone very short, some sort of strangely deformed man, or even a child to have been peering in through the glass.

Gerry closed his eyes and then opened them again. It hadn't gone away. It was still there.

He swallowed and got to his feet. He stared at the spot on the glass. He wasn't imaging it. There had to be a logical explanation. Probably just local kids, seeing what they could see while he was out and about. He wouldn't have even noticed if not for the rattling.

No, that had to be it. Kids. Definitely.

Five

It took a long time, but finally sleep overcame him again. He lay beneath the covers, still wrapped in his robe, listening to the sound of air rushing around the sides of the cottage, thinking about that face on the window. He hadn't bothered taking his robe off. Not that he was cold. It was more like an extra layer of security, a form of psychological protection against the imagined creatures wandering outside his house. He knew animals. He'd never seen something that looked quite like that. The noises, the darkness, they were simply playing tricks with his mind. After a time, he relaxed, huddled beneath the covers, the sound of the wind starting to sooth rather than disturb him, and he started to drift off.

He was in the wood. He recognised it, the colours, the scents. He was back in the dream, the same dream. The ground shifted, moving slowly beneath his feet, darkening, and changing hue, full of purples and blacks, mist wraiths streaming across the surface. He could hear the sound of air stirring through the branches around him. The sky was dark. The tree limbs moved, but it was more than just the wind. They had taken on a life of their own, twisting, stretching, and then withdrawing again. He could hear the sound of bark against bark, wood on wood as they scraped one across the other. He took a step forward, and then another. He knew he was heading somewhere, but he wasn't sure where. Everything was dim, fading in solidity, consumed by the gloom. The trees were mere shadows, but they stretched back and back forever. As he walked, the air stirred around him. There was a smell of vegetation, rich loamy earth. The ground felt springy beneath his feet. He took a step and then another. There were sounds now, strange shapes capering in the shadows, all angular features and pointed limbs and joints. They dashed about, quick, quick, almost too fast for the eye to see.

There came a whisper then. Someone was saying something. He couldn't quite make out the words. They seemed to be coming from all around him, drifting through the trees. He strained to make them out, and then he heard them, whispering.

"Come to me, Gerry," they said.

He looked up. Thin wisps of cloud trailed through the treetops, tinged with silver, like moonlight.

He was lost. He knew he was lost.

"Where are you?" he called.

From around him came the sound of laughter.

"Come to me." The frustration welled within him. He had to find the way. The words weren't whispered now. They were a voice, rich: a woman's voice. He turned one way and then another, seeking her out. He had to reach her.

He started trotting forward over the springy ground, ducking out of the way of branches, twigs that scratched at his face, reaching to claw him back. All around the creatures scampered, laughing, cackling. He held an arm up on front of his face to ward off the branches and pushed forward, desperate now to find her. He knew, deep within, that he *had* to find her.

Suddenly, there were no more branches, no more trees in his way. He was no longer running. He was standing still within a semi-clearing dominated by a huge ancient tree, its twisted branches woven into a crown above intertwined trunks. Further out towards the edges, they reached down, almost to the ground.

He knew this place, knew this tree. He'd been here before. It was the same tree, the same clearing. He could still sense movement all around him in the surrounding wood. Quick little dashes flickered in the corner of his eyes, and he could hear their scampering passage, if not quite see them.

And then, he was no longer alone.

Before him stood the young woman who had called herself Amanda. Even though it was dark, he could see her clearly, every detail.

"You came," she said. "You found me."

She smiled at him.

Gerry's gaze travelled over her perfect form, the green dress pressing against the curves of her body, the gentle curve of her lips, the pale alabaster skin, the slight dusting of freckles across her checks and that slim, fine nose. Her hair tumbled around her face, framing it, almost seeming to have a life of its own. She reached up with one hand towards his face.

"I'm glad," she said. "I knew you would. It was destined to be."

He was about to say something, his mouth open, forming the words and...

He was awake.

He could tell it was barely dawn. He blinked a couple of times and worked his mouth. For some reason, he was lying there with a throbbing erection. God, the dream hadn't even been sexual. Her image, though, that woman. Damn. Maybe his subconscious was trying to tell him something. Slowly he sat up, pushing back the covers, and pulled at the robe where it had bound itself around him in his sleep. He squeezed his eyes together tightly, worked some more saliva into his mouth and then shook his head. He could still see her there, saying those words, floating in his mind's eye. He realised he needed to do something about his bladder. Perhaps that would fix his other little problem as well. Taking a deep breath, he swung his feet out of the bed and padded out of the bedroom to attempt to make a start to the day.

Like any small village, Abbotsford had its good times and its bad, or its lean and fat as Ivy liked to think of them. There were times when the community grew and prospered and then the cycle would swing around again and things wouldn't go so well. For a few years, the population would grow and then it would dwindle in line with the good fortune or bad. Unfortunately, there was no tying that cycle of change to when *she* might be back again. You thought you could tell, and then things would suddenly start breaking or food going off in the fridge, the wind growing teeth as it were. It was not till one of the fat times that Ivy first had reason to apply her grandmother's collective wisdom. Once or twice during the intervening years, she thought she had cause, but then the winds had died away again and things returned to normal. Gradually, over the years, she had come to learn that it was like a season. You needed the fallow to help make the growth better, and when the bounty was good, then there must be payment. Some might think of it as retribution, but, in a way, she knew it was more like tribute. If they wanted to be taken care of, there would always be some sort of price to pay.

For the time being, there were five unattached young men in the area, not that it was much of a surprise. The pickings were a little slim around here for them to be otherwise. At the moment, they ranged in age from a mere eighteen years old to twenty-six. Knowing what they needed to do, it was hard. Eighteen was just so young. Two of them could be taken care of. The Bellows girl was about twenty-eight now, just a couple of years older than Christian Driver. So, that was one sorted out. Then there was Millie Foster. She was a bit young at sixteen, but there were worse things. She ticked them off in her head. That just left the three.

Funny, looking back, she remembered the way she'd first felt with her Alf. They'd ended up sharing so much together, both good and bad. It was that bond between them which over the years had drawn them steadily closer together. There had been sex, of course. They were a young man and a woman in their prime, thrust together and living in each other's pockets. They were man and wife after all. But it hadn't been about the physical side. That had just been there, part of the expectations of the day. Things were more open, more 'liberated' as they called it now, but still… She wondered how they were going to manage.

In the end, Alf had turned out to be her rock. He was her shoulder to cry on, her sympathetic ear, and there had been those times aplenty. She pictured his long gentle face and his big brown eyes. He'd be there for her in the following days, support whatever it was she decided to do, help convince the others that she was right.

Love was a funny thing the way it grew.

She drew back from her musings and turned her attention to the matter at hand. She had work to do, serious work.

It had been a bit of a day for Gerry, trundling around the narrow laneways and byways of Abbotsford and surrounds. He'd not quite settled from the dream, those strange marks on his windows, and he decided that he needed a drink. Well, maybe more than one. If he got a few too many under his belt, the cottage was within walking distance of the pub anyway. After the day's appointments, he'd not had the time to drop into Marchant's and, besides, he hardly wanted to do that just to ask Ivy some questions. Better if he had a few things to pick up, broach his queries in passing conversation. Heaven knew how Ivy would take it if he started showing a little too much interest. He didn't want to give her the opportunity. He pulled into the car park of the Fox and Hounds, locked the van up and headed inside. He paused for a moment, looking up at the sign. Funny, there might have been a hunting community around here once. There might have been lots of things. Given the name of the village, he supposed there might even have been an abbey here at some stage, though there was no sign of anything now, not even some crumbling ruins. Maybe some elevated Abbot had merely crossed a stream hereabouts and the name had simply stuck. He peered through the yellow thick glass in the door, but could make out nothing inside. As he did so, those strange marks on his own windows sprang to mind, and he lifted a hand, placing a palm flat upon the glass. They really had been just like that, someone peering into the cottage from the outside. He shook his head, pulled the heavy wooden door open and stepped in.

The Fox and Hounds was an old, old place. Gerry had no real idea how old, but inside it was all heavy wooden beams, low ceilings, and dark wood. He paused for a moment in the doorway, looking around the simple room. Round dark wood tables were surrounding by bentwood chairs, a few of the locals already in. One or two of them looked up at his entry, lifted their chins in recognition and then turned back to their drinks and their conversations. A couple of wooden booths ran along one of the walls with bench seats and tables between them. The lighting was low, yellowish, and the smell of what passed for the local ale filled the air. There was the smell of tobacco smoke as well, but he couldn't see any sign of anyone smoking. He guessed in a small place like this, the law was generally what you made of it. He crossed to the bar and pulled out one of the stools.

The publican, Gareth, Gerry thought his name was, stood in place behind the bar cleaning a glass. He wore a pale brown and green argyle vest over a mustardy coloured long-sleeved shirt. Large white whiskers sprouted from either side of his face, highlighting the ruddy complexion and perhaps cultivated as compensation for the thinning mop of white and grey hair on top of his round face. He watched as Gerry seated himself.

"So, what can I get our veterinary?" he asked.

"I'll have a pint, thanks," said Gerry. "Just the local."

The barman gave a couple of quick nods and placed his glass and towel down before getting a fresh one from the rack and moving over to pull a pint.

"Rough day?" he asked, looking up from the slowly filling glass. "You're looking a little worn."

"Not too bad," said Gerry. "Forgive me, but Gareth, isn't it?"

"Yes, that's right."

"No, just didn't sleep too well last night. Guess it's the wind."

"Mmm-hmm. The wind'll do that to you," he said. "It was up something fierce last night. You know what they say. Wind like that has teeth." He placed the pint down on the bar in front of Gerry.

Funny sort of thing to say, he thought.

"Get you anything else? Some crisps? Some nuts maybe? We've got these burger things here. I can heat one of them up for you if you like. Can't say that they're the best thing in the world, but they fill a hole. I'd do you a nice hot meal, but Sheila's not on tonight."

"No, no. That's fine. Though, if it's no bother, I wouldn't mind asking you a couple of questions. Mainly stuff about Abbotsford. I really haven't been here that long and a couple of things over the last few days have got me curious."

"If you like," said Gareth. "The Brandreth family have been in these parts for a long time. I probably know most of what there is to know."

"Okay…" said Gerry, pausing to take a couple of sips of his beer and collecting his thoughts.

"How old is Abbotsford, anyway?"

"Hmmm. The village, or something like it, has been here for a long, long time. Of course, it wasn't always Abbotsford. It had other names before that. But, as far as we know, there's people been living here for as long as there's been history and well before that." Gareth had returned to cleaning glasses, holding them up to the light and checking them as he talked.

"I thought so," said Gerry. "And what about the wood."

Gareth lowered the glass for a moment, peered over at Gerry. "The Lady's Wood. Why would you be asking about that?"

"Just curious, I suppose. The Lady's Wood. Never heard of it referred to as that."

"Oh, that's the name, right enough. That's an old, old place. Ancient. They say there used to be druids around in these parts. The Lady's Wood is supposed to be where they held their – what do you call them? – ceremonies or rituals or whatever. You hear all sorts of tales about that sort of stuff. A few of the folk round here say that it's a dark place. That it carries the memories of what went on there. Of course, that's long before any of us remember, long before any written history of such things. If there was anything, it goes way, way back. But you know people; they like to tell their tales. Nothing like a rousing bit of things that go bump in the night."

"Huh, interesting. I was up there yesterday. From what I could see it looked very old. Some of those trees…"

A slight frown flickered across Gareth's brow. "What were you doing up there?"

Gerry took another healthy swallow, wiped his mouth, and then plucked at his chin.

"Oh, I don't know," he said. "Curious, I suppose. A couple of things Ivy had said got me interested and I thought I'd go and have a look. Truth be told, I was up there just as much scavenging for firewood, not that I had much joy." He gave a short, self-deprecating laugh and drained the rest of his glass. Gareth was just standing there watching him, a slightly thoughtful expression on his face.

"Actually, I'll have another thanks, Gareth."

Gareth seemed to shake himself out of whatever he had been thinking about. "Right you are," he said and moved to pull another. "Let me get you a fresh glass."

Gerry waited for his order to be fulfilled and after taking a couple of thoughtful sips decided he might as well launch into his next question.

"You know Alf Wickford, right? Out on the farm on the other side of the wood?"

Gareth nodded his head in affirmation.

"Well, he doesn't have a daughter does he?"

"No. Not at all. Unless he's been keeping something secret from all of us for a long time."

"Well maybe a niece, or another relative who might be visiting?"

"Now why would you ask that? As far as I know, old Alf's been on his own for years, ever since Mabel passed. The kids are long gone. Both boys. Strapping young lads they were. Unlikely to see them back in Abbotsford."

"Well, funny thing... When I was out there, I met a young woman. She was a little odd, but I can't deny she was a bit of a looker."

"Odd, in what way?"

"Well, the things she said just seemed a little off is all. She said something about her name being Amanda and that she deserved to be loved."

Gareth went very still, stopping what he was doing in mid-wipe.

"Did she have red hair, by any chance?" he said slowly.

"She did at that, and deep, thick red hair. Couldn't miss it. Sounds like you might know her. Do you know where she lives ? Not that there's probably much hope for me, but..."

Gareth slowly lowered the glass. "You say she spoke to you."

"That's right."

"Take my word for it. You want to stay away from that one. And best we don't say any more on the subject. Best not to talk about her at all. If you take my advice, you won't mention this to anyone else hereabouts neither." He fixed Gerry with a stern look. "Heed what I'm telling you, young Mr. Summerfield. It's for you own good."

Gerry narrowed his eyes for a moment, trying to take it all in.

"Okay," he said reluctantly, the word drawn out.

"I'm deadly serious, young man. I wouldn't say this lightly."

Gerry nodded slowly.

"Right." He finished the drink quickly and placed the empty glass down on the bar. "Right," he said again, "I'd better be off."

He was conscious of Gareth watching him as he headed for the door, saying nothing.

Six

That night, even after a couple of pints to act as a makeshift soporific, his unease remained. The wind, the faces, the dream, all of it was adding up to a sense of disquiet that just wouldn't leave him. After he got home, he'd paced around the confines of the cottage listening to the wind worrying at the walls and roof, buffeting the place as if it wanted to get in. Now and again, he shot nervous glances at the windows, expecting at any moment to see some sort of misshapen face peering in at him. He'd almost seen them in his dreams, could almost put a shape to them. Almost. After a while, he simply stopped looking at the windows. With the lights on inside, he couldn't see what was outside the cottage anyway. He foraged in the kitchen and the fridge, not finding anything aside from some stale bread and old cheese, so he set about making himself cheese on toast with a touch of tabasco and a dash of Worcestershire sauce. It wasn't much, but it would do to stave off the peckishness that always sat with him after a couple of pints. By the state of his larder, he'd need to pay Marchant's a visit after all, but the publican's warning had stayed with him. He wasn't sure now whether he should mention anything to Ivy at all. In the end, he'd decided to leave the van at the pub, so he'd have to walk down that way anyway in the morning to pick it up. He could decide then whether or not to say anything to her.

After he'd put away his things, he made his way into the living room and slumped in front of the box for a while, but couldn't concentrate. There was nothing much on that he felt like watching anyway, and he had it on just as a distraction, just to provide some background noise and familiar moving colours and shapes that weren't going to make his skin prickle. Eventually, he headed off to bed.

He was dreaming again. He was asleep and dreaming, but he knew he was dreaming at the same time. He was in the wood. He recognised it, the colours, the scents. Though he was back in the same dream, there was something different and it was more than just his awareness of the dream state. The ground was shifting, just like the last time, moving slowly beneath his feet, darkening, and changing hue, full of purples and blacks. Tendrils of mist crept across its surface. A breeze whispered through the branches. Above him everything was in darkness. How could he be remembering a dream inside a dream? He didn't understand. The branches were moving again, on their own. It was not just the wind moving them. They flexed back and forth, growing, and stretching, then withdrawing again. As he had the last time, he took a step forward, and then another. He was heading somewhere, but he didn't know where. All around him, gloom swallowed detail, consuming substance and form. Again came the rich heady scent of plants and of deep earth. Each step sprang as the ground gave, and then pushed back beneath his feet. Then came the familiar sounds, the strange shapes cavorting in the darkness, all angles, and joints where there should be none, seen and yet unseen, flickering at the edges of his perception.

He had been expecting it this time: the whisper, the words indistinct. The sound came from every direction.

"Come to me, Gerry," she said.

He looked up. Thin wisps of cloud trailed through the treetops, tinged with silver, like moonlight.

A sense of desperation grew within him. He didn't know where she was, but he needed to reach her. The need was throbbing within him. He was lost. He knew he was lost.

"Where are you?" he called.

Laughter echoed from the trees.

"Come to me," came the voice, her voice.

Desperation rose inside him. He had to find the way. He had to locate the path that would lead him to her. Everything depended on it.

He started trotting forward over the springy ground, ducking out of the way of branches, twigs that reached out to claw him back. All around, the creatures scampered, laughing, cackling. He held an arm up on front of his face to ward off the branches and pushed forward, desperate to find her.

Then, as before, there were no more branches, nothing in his way. He stood in an open clearing, but this time it was different. There was no great tree standing in the middle. All around, thick trunks, one against the other, masked everything from view apart from the clearing. He looked up, and the sky was clear, stars shining down on him with a soft light. Leaves covered the ground in a soft carpet. And then there, standing in the clearing's centre, she appeared. She beckoned to him.

"Come to me, Gerry," she said. Her voice was rich, full of promise.

Slowly he stepped forward. The sense of relief at having found her was washing over him. As he neared, she lifted one hand, held it out towards his cheek, and then rested it gently against his skin. It was smooth, warm, and smelled of something floral, or perhaps herbal. Suddenly, he was filled with expectation. She was beautiful, gorgeous, and she was here with him. He felt himself reacting.

"Don't you want me, Gerry?" she said.

Her deep green eyes fixed on his, she slipped off one shoulder of her dress.

"Don't you desire me? Am I not everything you ever wanted?"

"Oh god, yes," the words struggled from his lips.

She slipped off the other shoulder and the dress fell to the ground about her ankles. Beneath, she wore nothing. His eyes drank in her form, his breath coming in shallow gasps. She was perfect. Perfect in a way that he had never imagined.

As she drew him down to the carpet of leaves, she whispered in his ear.

"Do you love me?" she said.

He could hardly think. "What?" he barely managed, forcing the word out as a breath.

"Tell me," she said.

Words of any form were beyond his imagining at that moment. She was unfastening his clothes, pulling them away from his body.

They lay naked now, together, surrounded by trees and darkness, but it was as if they were illuminated, bathed in a gentle glow in the clearing's centre. She moved across his body and spoke gently in his ear, her voice husky, breathy.

"Tell me now," she said. "Do you love me?"

And in that moment, before he had a chance to speak, he was awake again.

He sat up in the darkness, his hand held across his mouth.

"Oh god," he said. The words came out as a whisper, barely muffled by his hand. He took a few short, shallow breaths and then leaned back, his face up towards the ceiling. What the hell was happening? What the hell was happening to him? Something wasn't right. That much was sure.

"Oh god," he breathed again.

He doubted very much that he was going to get any more sleep tonight.

"You have to understand. Two of my kegs went off this morning and I lost the generator too. Can't see what I need to do to fix it."

Gareth stood in front of her counter, his big red face more florid than usual.

"And there are other things," he said.

He seemed to be waiting for some sort of response. "Yes, I know, Gareth," said Ivy. "You don't have to tell me, but there are things to decide, things to take care of. If we are going to do this, then we have to do it right. We only have a couple of choices at the moment, and we need to make the decision between us. We can try to protect them, or... Well, you know she's a jealous one."

"I really don't think we have much choice, Ivy. I really don't."

"And why is that?"

"Damned fool boy was in the wood."

Ivy set her lips in a thin line. "I see," she said.

"Not only that," Gareth continued. "She's noticed him. Said he'd talked to her. Met her out by Old Alf's place."

"Damn it all," she said quietly.

"I know."

"Well you're right. I can see that. We can't do anything without letting the others know, though. It's only right. I'd talked a bit about the possibility with Tom, but I didn't know that. When did it happen?

"Two days ago, by all accounts."

"That would tie in with the happenings. She's awake right enough. I don't remember her talking to anyone before this, though. She must really be hungry. No one else has mentioned anything, have they?"

Gareth shook his head. "Not a peep."

Ivy drew a deep breath through her nose and pressed her mouth tightly shut in a grimace. She had hoped it might not come to this, but there was no escaping it now. With a tut, she started tapping on the glass countertop with the fingers of one hand.

"All right," she said finally. "I'll let Tom know. You talk to the others. I would, but I have to look up a few things. It's been far too long, and you know what happens if we don't get this right."

Gareth nodded a few times, clearly processing what she was saying.

"Right then," he said finally. "I'll be off."

"And be smart about it," said Ivy as he turned and made for the door.

She stood there at her counter, slowly shaking her head for a while before she turned to make her way upstairs.

"You know why you're all here," said Ivy.

Mary bustled out of the kitchen bearing a large serving plate before her. It was her place that they were meeting at.

"I got the buns in," she said.

"Very thoughtful of you, Mary," Ivy told her. She reached for the teapot and poured herself a cup.

"Feel free to help yourselves, everyone," said Mary.

Around the large dining table sat Ivy, Mary, Tom Mills, William Morrison, and Gareth Brandreth from the Fox and Hounds. They mumbled their thanks to Mary and helped themselves to cups of tea and sticky buns.

"Where's Charlie?" asked Ivy.

"Said something about having to run an errand," William offered. "Said he'd be along as soon as he could manage it and not to wait."

"Right then," said Ivy. She lifted her cup and took a sip. The others were watching her expectantly. Slowly she placed the cup back down on her saucer and, using both hands, smoothed the tablecloth with her palms.

William fumbled around in his pocket and dug out his old briar pipe, held it up in front of him. "Does anyone mind?"

"I'd rather you didn't, Bill," said Ivy.

He cleared his throat, grimaced, and placed the old pipe back in his pocket.

Ivy nodded and then looked around each of their faces in turn. There were others in the village, of course, but assembled here were the core, counting of course the absent Charlie. Some of the others outside the group knew that they were meeting and would know why as well, but they'd be happy enough to trust in the wisdom of those gathered around this table. They were the closest thing to what would have been village elders in earlier times. She trusted these few, and it was not the first time they'd been called upon to meet. It was clear they needed to do something this time, that there wasn't much of a choice.

"Well, we don't need Charlie to get underway. It should be fairly obvious to all of you where we are at the moment."

"I've seen the signs," said William.

"So have I," added Mary.

"But you're the keeper of the lore, Ivy," said Gareth, shaking his head, and pursing his lips so that his big white mutton chops seemed to stick further out from his head. He took in a deep breath and scratched his throat. "You know better than all of us how bad it's going to be."

Ivy held her cup with both hands, looking down into the remaining milky tea and not lifting her gaze. "I think it's going to be very bad unless we do something quickly."

William reached into his pocket, pulled out his pipe, looked at it, frowned, and then put it away again.

"But what choice do we have?" asked Mary, reaching for another bun.

"Well, there's two right now, no more," said Tom. "Ivy and I have discussed it a bit, but we wanted to put it in front of you as well."

"So, let's hear them," said William.

"You know as well as I do, Bill, as well as all of us do." Ivy looked at him sternly. "Don't pretend you don't."

"Just so we're clear," said Tom. "There's the Stubbins boy, and then there's the veterinary. That's our lot. Not as if our population's growing for now."

Gareth grunted. "Is it any wonder?" he said.

"It can't be young Simon. Think of his old mum," said Mary. "We need to look after our own, don't we?" She looked around at each of their faces in turn.

"Be a shame, though," said Gareth. "He's only just got here. Barely got his feet wet. Not as if he's trouble or anything."

"Well, you come up with another suggestion, Gareth Brandreth," said Ivy. "Especially with what you told me. She's seen him." She looked around the table at each of them in turn, driving home the point. "She's noticed him. She knows. Damn fool boy was off mucking around in the wood. Perhaps someone should have taken the trouble to warn him, but it's a bit late for that now."

Gareth merely gazed down at the table and shook his head.

The others looked around at each other and then turned back to Ivy. Not a one of them had anything else to offer. As usual, it was going to fall on Ivy's shoulders and hers alone. There were things about that that she liked a little, but at the same time, there were things about it that she hated.

"Right we are then," said Ivy, placing her cup back down on the saucer and laying her hands flat upon the table. "That's where we are. In the meantime, I'll try and come up with some other possibility. As you say, Gareth, it'd be a shame, but I don't think we have much of a choice. We know what happens if we do nothing and things have already started to take their own course."

Just then there was a knock at the door. Mary excused herself and went to answer. There were voices and then moments later, she was back, leading Charlie in with his thick glasses, flat cap, and stick.

"What have I missed?" he said from the doorway.

"Nice of you to turn up, Charlie," said Ivy. "We've just been discussing options. Mary can fill you in. In the meantime, I have some things to attend to at home. I need to run through the things we'll need. It's been a long while since the last time. A very long while. It's what, nearly eighteen years now?"

William gave a confirming nod.

"If I need anything else from any of you, I'll be sure to let you know."

With that, she excused herself and made her way out, leaving all of them sitting there at the table, saying nothing. She was sure that the talking would start up as soon as she had left.

As she headed back up the High Street, Ivy's thoughts were conflicted. The temptation to do nothing was so easy. In fact, that was her more natural urge, but she knew what would happen if they did. Every one of them, the whole village, would reap the reward, and a bitter reward it would be. No, she simply could not let that happen again. There really was no other answer, despite what she had told the others, and deep within she knew it. She had seen what had happened before. Gareth, Tom, and William had all taken part in those events as well. Mary was a relative newcomer. She'd come to Abbotsford by marriage. Charlie had been around then, too, but who knew what he had noticed or hadn't. Charlie sort of lived in a little world of his own. He'd been a stonemason once, and a damned good one. Ever since he'd retired, though, he seemed to have drifted a little. He always seemed to be running these mysterious little errands, whatever they were all about. It was better just to let him get on with it, she supposed. Who knew what went on inside that strange little head of his?

Back at home, she spent a while sitting at her kitchen table just staring off into the distance before she set about the task at hand. Her thoughts had drifted to the one person who was missing from their little circle. In her mind's eye, she reached up to cup that familiar face, always familiar even after all these years, the changes that came with them. She missed him so much, missed the sound of his voice, the smell of him, the feeling of his arm around her back. Her Alf had been her everything. Not at the beginning, of course, but that was what it had become. And now, even after all this time, there was an ache inside her from where he was gone. Yes, she knew he was gone, knew he wouldn't be back. Who could tell if there was something after, whether she'd see him again? It didn't matter, though. He was still with her and he'd always let her know that what she was doing was right, just as he always had. She took a deep breath and held it before slowly letting it out again. Back to the here and now, she thought. Things needed doing. The whole village was relying on her now. She needed to make a start.

Seven

The lack of sleep, even though it had only really been a couple of nights, was starting to wear on him. It was more than sleeplessness, he supposed. It was the weather, the wind. He remembered reading somewhere once that constant wind rushing past you generates static electricity in the body, making you tense. He wasn't sure how true that was, but it certainly felt like it. Earlier that afternoon, he'd had a rep from a veterinary supply company visit. They sat together in the surgery as he ran through the virtues of a range of products. Gerry had barely listened the whole way through. In the end, as much to get rid of the fellow as anything else, he'd agreed to trial a couple of the samples, but nothing much else. He couldn't even remember now which products he'd ended up with. Apart from that it was a quiet day. Quiet, in terms of appointments. The wind was still making its presence well and truly felt. He tried catching up on a couple of journals, but couldn't concentrate on those either. He didn't know how many times he read and re-read the same paragraph in one of the articles before finally giving up. Every time he had a few moments free, images from the dream would swim up into his thoughts, distracting him. Slowly, slowly, the afternoon wore on, and as it did, he felt increasingly more fraught. He needed to find a solution soon, or he was going to end up a wreck.

Later in the afternoon, he tried to distract himself by going for a walk. That turned out to be not a very good idea. It was still nasty out. The wind plucked and played with him, tore at his coat, and made it flap around his legs. He walked on, head down, grimacing against the buffeting gusts and stealing the occasional glance up in the direction of the wood. Lady's Wood. That's what Gareth the publican had called it. Maybe it was the things he'd said that had prompted the dreams. That, and the fact that it had been some time since he'd actually been 'with' anyone in that way. Certainly that last dream, anyway. After about ten minutes, Gerry conceded defeat and retreated back to the cottage. It was almost as if the weather was conspiring to keep him at home.

He was hunkered down in the kitchen, peering into the refrigerator trying to decide what he might make for dinner, when a knock at the door surprised him. With a frown, he got to his feet and headed out to see who it might possibly be. Perhaps there was an emergency with a local pet, but you would have thought they could have telephoned. He opened the door find Ivy standing there. Nor was she alone. There were two others with her, a woman he'd seen around but didn't know her name, and the local butcher, Morrison, Gerry thought his name was. They all three looked at him expectantly. Ivy wore a floral frock and a cardigan. The other woman had on a dreadful pink sort of tracksuit affair and she held a covered dish in front of her. The man stood there in a tweed jacket and corduroy trousers with a large well-used pipe clamped firmly between his teeth.

"Um, hello," he said.

"Hello, Gerry," said Ivy, with a big smile. "We thought we'd pop round and see how you were getting on. I guess you know William, our local butcher."

William raised a finger to his forehead.

"And this is Mary."

"I've brought cakes," said the other one.

"Um, right," said Gerry. "You'd, um, better come in then."

"Very kind," said Ivy. She turned briefly to the man. "And you can put that stinky thing away, William Morrison," she said.

He took the pipe from his mouth and sheepishly slipped it into his pocket.

Gerry was at a complete loss for something to say, and instead made do with, "Through this way," standing back and holding out a hand in the direction of the living room.

"No that's all right," said Ivy. "Been here plenty of times before when Arthur was still here. We know our way."

Gerry followed as they filed into the living room, and stood in the doorway numbly. He had absolutely no idea what had prompted this little group to descend upon him.

"I'll take these out to the kitchen, shall I? Find some plates..." said Mary.

"Yes, right," said Gerry, still struggling. "I supposed you'd better sit."

Ivy nodded. "Thank you. And why don't you join us?"

"Right, of course," said Gerry, and he positioned himself in the big old armchair as both Ivy and William settled on the couch. Ivy sat watching him. William was gazing around the room, looking fidgety. He would reach for his pocket and then bring his hands back and clasp them in front of him, leaning forward, his elbows on his thighs. Gerry was a little lost for something to say.

"I know this might seem like it's come out of nowhere," said Ivy. "But we thought we'd see how you're settling in. Probably should have done it sooner, but, well, you know, better late than never, eh?"

Gerry gave her a fixed smile and nodded.

"Just, well, these last few days," she continued, "we've had concerns. You've been looking very haggard, and we just wanted to make sure everything is all right with you. Just think of it as neighbourly concern. Not exactly the welcome wagon, I know. A bit late for that really, but nevertheless..."

"Um, well…"

"Here we go," said Mary, emerging from the kitchen with a handful of small plates and the larger dish that she'd brought with her, uncovered now to reveal a selection of frosted cupcakes. She placed both down on the coffee table. "Plenty to go around," she said, and proceeded to take a plate and load a couple of the cakes on to it for herself.

"What about a nice cup of tea," said Ivy. "Now I'm sure you've a pot and some cups. Let me make us some. You stay right there, Gerry and I'll look after it."

"I don't know if I have enough teacups, but there's some mugs in the kitchen cabinet," he said. Things were very rapidly slipping out of his control.

"Right we are then," said Ivy. "You stay here and have a little chat with William and Mary, while I sort everything out." She gave a little chuckle. "Anybody would think they were furniture," she said. "William and Mary. Well they're definitely not royalty."

William responded with an amused grunt.

"Anyway, how do you take it? I know these two's order."

"Um, milk and two, thanks," said Gerry.

Ivy got to her feet, dusted off her thighs and bustled off into the kitchen.

"So," William started in as soon as she had left them. "What have you been getting up to, outside of your work time that is. Not all that much to do for a young man such as yourself hereabouts. Of course there's the pub, but these days it tends to be full of boring old farts like me."

"I don't know," said Gerry. "I seem to be able to keep myself amused. I've got my journals. There's the TV, and the internet. I read. Been doing a bit of exploring lately too. Finding out a bit about the local area."

"What about friends?" said Mary.

"Well, not really any yet, I suppose," he responded.

She went all coy then. "Any young flames?"

"Chance would be a fine thing," he said. "I did meet someone the other day. She seemed okay, but for some reason I got warned off her by our local publican."

"Did he say anything about why?"

"He probably had his reasons," said Ivy, emerging from the kitchen. She placed a mug of tea down in front of William and one in front of Mary then retreated to the kitchen again. "Our Gareth knows quite a bit about what's going around in these parts. You should probably heed what he has to say. He hears a lot from behind that bar of his," she said from the doorway before stepping out of sight again and busying herself with the remaining teas.

"Hum," said William. "Tell me, Gerry. Apart from all that, how are you finding the place?"

"Oh, it's a nice town," said Gerry. "Nice people."

"Yes, they are," said Ivy, returning with his tea and one for herself and then sitting herself back down on the couch. "Salt of the earth, our people.

Gerry reached forward, grabbed himself a plate and one of the cakes, then took a sip of his tea. Strong and sweet, as he liked it.

"I probably can't see myself staying here long term though, truth be told," he said. "I've got time for other things before I think about settling. And, it's a bit like you said, William. Not that much here for me."

"Apart from that redhead, right?" said William.

Gerry took another sip and then frowned. He didn't recall saying anything about a redhead.

"Um, right," he said, processing that. He sipped at the tea as he considered. This was a village. They all probably talked to each other, discussed every find point of everyone's lives in minute detail. He looked at William, then at Mary. The man was fidgeting again, and Mary was reaching for another of her cakes, focussed on her choice, fingers hovering over one and then the other. He looked over at Ivy. She wasn't drinking her tea. She wasn't saying anything. She was simply sitting there, unmoving, watching him intently.

Suddenly he felt immensely tired.

Unable to help himself, he gave a huge yawn.

"Oh, I'm sorry," he said. "I just don't seem to have been able to sleep that much these last few days."

He punctuated that with another yawn, which just welled up and took him over.

"Gee. Sorry," he said again and shook his head, blinking.

Again a yawn overtook him, and very, very carefully, he placed his mug back down on the table.

It seemed as if everything had slowed down, as if he was moving through a thick invisible soup.

"Gerry?" He heard Ivy's voice. He thought it was Ivy, but it seemed to be coming from so, so far away.

Gradually his eyelids started to drift closed. He tried to force them open once or twice, but then simply gave up.

None of it seemed to matter anymore, really.

Slowly, his head muzzy, Gerry struggled back to consciousness. There was a pounding in his right temple and something deep in the back of his skull. He shook his head, tried to move, but there was something stopping him. He could hear voices. His mouth was dry. He tried working it to regain some moisture, but at that moment realised there was something bound around it, stopping him moving his lips, his mouth. He tried pushing his tongue against it, tasting cloth. A smell surrounded his face and something blocked his sight. He knew that smell. Hessian. His head was covered in a hessian sack. What the hell? He tried calling out, but whatever was covering his mouth muffled his voice. Something hard and round pressed up against his back. His arms were wrapped around it, behind him. He tried pulling at them, but they were too tightly bound. Small glimmers of light flickered through the weave that covered his eyes. Fires. Firelight, or something similar. He could see strands of the weave, like spiderwebs made white in the flickering light.

"Hey!" he tried calling, but his voice was distorted into a muffle yell. "Hey!" He tried again.

Still there were voices. He couldn't recognise them. They weren't words. It was a low chant.

He struggled again, trying to twist free, but his bonds were tight. The light through the weave was dancing wildly. He could hear the wind. Not fires. They were torches. He had the impression of a shadowy shape moving closer, presumably a person. He strained, cried out again, but it had no effect. Whoever it was reached up, pulled the sack from his head and he could see again. He blinked against the light. He could smell the burning. Squinting around, he made out several people, some holding torches, all dressed in the same in shapeless grey shifts. On their heads, they wore woven branches. Then he recognised some of the faces. He knew these people. They were from the village. What the hell was going on? His attention drew back to the person in front of him, holding the limp sack in one hand, looking at him. It was Ivy. Ivy Marchant from the shop.

He tried to force her name through the gag, but it came out as a shapeless noise. Then he merely yelled. No words, just sound. He felt the panic start to rise in earnest. His breath became short, a coldness settling deep in the pit of his stomach. What the hell were they doing? What was going on?

He frowned and shook his head, and then he realised through the panic that he recognised this place. He, *they*, were in the wood. It was dark, but he could see by the light of the torches that this was where he had been before, the old tree with the hollow at the centre of its trunk. The clearing that was not a clearing. The flickering torches made the trunk dance with grotesque shapes. All around, the villagers kept up their low chant. Above him, the branches danced in the swirling wind.

Again Gerry twisted, writhing against the post that held him, but he was bound tight. Again, he yelled wordlessly against the cloth that was pulled firmly across his mouth and holding his head in place. He felt he was going to lose control of his bladder, but then something else other than panic began to grow inside him. Slowly, slowly, anger started to rise, growing steadily inside, threatening to burst forth, but there was nowhere for it to go, nowhere for him to go. He wanted to reach out and wipe that calm expression from Ivy's face. His jaw clenched and he yelled again, pulling futilely at his bindings.

Ivy lifted something, a small bowl, and with her thumb she dipped and then reached out, painting something slick upon his forehead. There was a smell then, of herbs, or leaves or something similar, and a warm slick trail that trickled down his forehead and along one side of his nose. He still didn't understand what was going on, but he didn't like it one bit. And he was completely powerless to do anything about it. Again, he struggled against his bonds. Once more Ivy reached up. This time she held a woven circlet of twigs and leaves. With both hands, she placed it upon his head. Then she spoke.

"Gerry Summerfield," she said. "Now, as is right, your heart belongs to her."

She bowed her head, placed the bowl down at his feet and then stepped back, joining the rest of them. He looked around, his eyes wide. It had to be most of the adult members of the village standing there. She took up the low chant. He couldn't recognise the words. It wasn't Latin. He didn't think it sounded like Greek. What the hell were they saying? What were they doing?

He tried catching Ivy's eyes, tried to frown a query at her, but then his attention was drawn away as all everyone turned towards the tree. He shifted his gaze to follow them and then suddenly, he went cold again, stopping his struggling, his jaw slack beneath the gag.

And in that moment, in the clearing, the wind stopped.

Something stirred within the darkness in front of him, the black hollow that sat at the centre of that huge old tree.

All around the edges of the space, the air rushed through branches, shaking them, swirling around the clearing's edges and he caught something else there, rapid jerky motions, shapes, dashing around. He thought he caught a face, or what looked like a face, all angular and pointed in ways a face should not be, and then it was gone again into the swirling wind. There might be limbs and arms and hands, but he couldn't be sure.

Within that dark archway at the tree's centre there was movement. At first, he thought he'd imagined it, but then he could tell for sure. A shape began to resolve itself in the darkness, and then a figure ducked beneath the top edge and then slowly straightened. He knew her. That perfect face, pale skin, the red hair, a slight smile painted across her lips, the green dress, flickering black and shadowed in the torchlight. It was the young woman, Amanda. And yet...

Never taking her gaze from his face, she walked slowly forward, unhurriedly, step after measured step. Strange he hadn't noticed it before, but her feet were bare.

All around him, the villagers stood silent, watching, torches held beside them. Everything was silent. Just for a moment, a breath of air slipped across the clearing, moving through the branches, and rattling them slightly. As she grew closer, there was a smell of earth, old leaves, vegetation, rich wood, filling the air around him.

Again, he tried to force a yell, but it came out as a hoarse, muffled cry. She stood there in front of him, studying his face, as if curious, interested. She tilted her head to one side, reached up, placed a palm against his cheek. He tried to pull away, tried to shrink back, but there was nothing that he could do. Slowly, she lowered her hand straightened her head, and then she smiled.

"Yes," she said. "He will do." Still she appeared to study his face.

Around him he could sense a slight stir from the assembled people.

"I know this one," she said. "He's been here before."

Then she leaned in closer.

"Do you love me?" she said quietly, almost a whisper.

Gerry's eyes went wide. Was she mad? Was he mad? All this was crazy.

"Do you love me?" she said again, louder this time.

This couldn't be happening. It just couldn't. Did this woman really expect him to answer her?

He looked into those eyes, green, so green, and as he looked, they seemed to glow. He blinked a couple of times. Still he struggled, never breaking her gaze, pushing against his bonds, feeling the hard post, because that's what it had to be, digging into his back. The makeshift crown upon his head moved a little, jagging at his forehead, breaking skin. He could feel a trickle of something else now upon his face. She was watching his efforts interestedly, curiously, but seemingly unmoved by his plight. There was a twitch at her lips, and those impossible green eyes grew wider, deeper, the colour intensifying, growing with an inner light. And then, as he watched, something else started to happen. Could he be imagining it, but was she growing?

They'd drugged him, that much was clear, but was he hallucinating now too? He stopped his movement, froze. It couldn't be happening. But it was. She was growing larger, the eyes, wider, rounder, and something else was happening too. Her skin was changing, turning brown, no, brown, and green at the same time, taking on a different texture. Still smooth, but harder, rounder. What looked like thick ropes of muscle rippled beneath the surface of her face. Her hair streamed out, bound together in ropes and strands that thickened, grew branches, leaves, green, barbed. And still the changes went on. Her arms grew, the dress merging with the flesh beneath. Thick, knotted, the limbs stretched out and out, hands becoming longer, the fingers pointed, sharp. Her body became rounder, wider, and formed columns of solidity that wove one around the other. Her skin, if it was skin, became darker still, touched with strands of yellow-green. There were no legs any more, just a collection of solid trunks, fused together and yet mobile. What had been feet and toes now stretched out across the ground like roots, yet they were in constant motion, feeling at the ground as if tasting it.

Her face was long now, her lips hard. Her eyes had grown large, round, though still that impossible green, and within their depths swam golden motes. She opened that mouth wide, and within it were vines, twisting. Gerry was transfixed by her gaze, held like an insect. All volition seemed to have flowed away, out of his limbs, deserted him. Futilely, he tried to cry out again, and then she laughed. It was deep and rich, and he felt it rush through him.

"Do you love me?" her voice rang through him. Though it was different, changed, it was still her, still the same words. "I know you do. I have felt it."

She stood there above him, looking down at him, waving a little as if pushed by an invisible breeze, considering.

"Then your heart belongs to me," she said.

With that, she drew back her arm, and then plunged it forward, the sharp hard fingers held together, and just as quickly, she drew it back, holding something now, wet, dripping. Slowly, slowly, she lifted it to her mouth.

Gerry felt the impact, as if a wall had slammed into him. There wasn't any pain, not at first. And then it blossomed, unfolding like a sharp-edged chrysanthemum inside his chest, along with the darkness that started gently draping across his vision.

And then, there was simply nothing.

The villagers maintained the circle, heads bowed until she was done. One or two of them ventured surreptitious glances, Ivy among them. She watched the tall sinuous form, working, moving in quick staccato movements, sometimes blurring, too fast to track, arms moving, garlanded head dipping and then lifting again. A flash here, a darting movement there. By the time she had sated herself, there was little to see of what had once been Gerry Summerfield.

Pity, thought Ivy. *He'd seemed a nice enough young man, but, well, needs must.*

The Lady was withdrawing back into herself now, changing, the branches shrinking, losing the aspect of wood and leaves. Gradually, she grew smaller, contracting until a sweet unassuming-looking redheaded young woman stood in front of the now mostly-empty post. Without looking at any of them, she turned, strolled unhurriedly towards that chamber of dark in the middle of the tree's multiple conjoined trunks. There had been no sign of her work upon her face and hands, nor on the green dress that she habitually wore. They waited hesitantly for a while, and then one by one they started to douse their torches. Bit by bit, the darkness descended around them. Ivy stepped over to the clearing's edge, retrieved her handbag and dug around inside it for the heavy duty torch she carried for just such an eventuality. The moon was only half full and the light filtering through the twisted branches was silvery and wan. The others were starting to wander off in ones and twos.

"Mind how you go then, Mary, William," she said to a couple of the figures, shapes there was no mistaking. Bill lifted a hand in acknowledgement and continued into the darkness between the trees.

"Well, that's that for another year then," said Tom, wandering up to her. "At least for this year."

"For now," said Ivy. "Who knows how long till she's back again."

"Time to find ourselves a new veterinary, I suppose," said Tom.

Ivy looked away, over in the direction of the grand old tree, at the deeper darkness lying at the trunk's centre. It was all still now. The wind that had whipped through the branches above them had died away completely.

"Maybe this time we might see if we can get a woman."

"Aye. Might be best," said Tom thoughtfully. "He'd barely found his way around."

Ivy pursed her lips, scanning what she could see of the clearing in the shadow and gloom. "You'll need to come out in the morning and clean things up a bit," she said.

"It'll keep a day or two. Not like anyone's going to say anything about it."

Ivy said nothing, merely returned her attention to cleaning her hands. All in all, it was a messy business. She looked down at the spots on her grey shift and tutted to herself. There was nothing for it – she was *definitely* going to have to soak it now.

Of course, they'd have to think up a story on the off chance that somebody asked, but she had no concern that they would all keep it straight. He'd seemed like a bit of a loner, after all. But in the meantime, she needed to get home and do something about these clothes.

She sighed. Life goes on.

Life simply goes on.

About the Author

Jay Caselberg is an Australian author who also claims British nationality, based in Europe. His work, often tending to the dark side, has appeared in many venues worldwide and in several languages. His most recent novel was Empties. More can be found at http://www.caselberg.net

Selected bibliography:

Jack Stein
1. Wyrmhole (2003)
2. Metal Sky (2004)
3. The Star Tablet (2005)
4. Wall of Mirrors (2006)

Angel on the Beach (2010)
Binary (2013)
Unnatural Conditions (2013)
Empties (2015)

Newcon Press Novellas, Set 2

Simon Clark / Alison Littlewood / Sarah Lotz / Jay Caselberg

Cover art by Vincent Sammy

Case of the Bedevilled Poet ~ His life under threat, poet Jack Crofton flees through the streets of war-torn London. He seeks sanctuary in a pub and falls into company with two elderly gentlemen who claim to be the real Holmes and Watson. Unconvinced but desperate, Jack shares his story, and Holmes agrees to take his case…

Cottingley ~ A century after the world was rocked by news that two young girls had photographed fairies in the sleepy village of Cottingley, we finally learn the true nature of these fey creatures. Correspondence has come to light; a harrowing account written by village resident Lawrence Fairclough that lays bare the fairies' sinister malevolence.

Body in the Woods ~ When an old friend turns up on Claire's doorstep one foul night and begs for her help, she knows she should refuse, but she owes him and, despite her better judgement, finds herself helping to bury something in the woods. Will it stay buried, and can Claire live with the knowledge of what she did that night?

The Wind ~ Having moved to Abbotsford six months ago, Gerry reckons he's getting used to country life and the rural veterinary practice he's taken on. Nothing prepared him, though, for the strange wind that springs up to stir the leaves in unnatural fashion, nor for the strikingly beautiful woman the villagers are so reluctant to talk about…

NewCon Press Novellas, Set 1

Alastair Reynolds – The Iron Tactician

A brand new stand-alone adventure featuring the author's long-running character Merlin. The derelict hulk of an old swallowship found drifting in space draws Merlin into a situation that proves far more complex than he ever anticipated.

Released December 2016

Simon Morden – At the Speed of Light

A tense drama set in the depths of space; the intelligence guiding a human-built ship discovers he may not be alone, forcing him to contend with decisions he was never designed to face.

Released January 2017

Anne Charnock – The Enclave

A new tale set in the same milieu as the author's debut novel *A Calculated Life*". The Enclave: bastion of the free in a corporate, simulant-enhanced world...shortlisted for the 2013 Philip K. Dick Award.

Released February 2017

Neil Williamson – The Memoirist

In a future shaped by omnipresent surveillance, why are so many powerful people determined to wipe the last gig by a faded rock star from the annals of history? What are they afraid of?

Released March 2017

All cover art by Chris Moore

www.newconpress.co.uk

IMMANION PRESS

Purveyors of Speculative Fiction

The Lightbearer by Alan Richardson

Michael Horsett parachutes into Occupied France before the D-Day Invasion. He is dropped in the wrong place, miles from the action, badly injured, and totally alone. He falls prey to two Thelemist women who have awaited the Hawk God's coming, attracts a group of First World War veterans who rally to what they imagine is his cause, is hunted by a troop of German Field Police who are desperate to find him, and has a climactic encounter with a mutilated priest who believes that Lucifer Incarnate has arrived...

The Lightbearer is a unique gnostic thriller, dealing with the themes of Light and Darkness, Good and Evil, Matter and Spirit.

"The Lightbearer is another shining example of Alan Richardson's talent as a story-teller. He uses his wide esoteric knowledge to produce a story that thrills, chills and startles the reader as it radiates pure magical energy. An unusual and gripping war story with more facets than a star sapphire." – Mélusine Draco, author of *"Aubry's Dog"* and *"Black Horse, White Horse".* ISBN: 978-1-907737-63-3 £11.99 $18.99

Dark in the Day, Ed. by Storm Constantine & Paul Houghton

Weirdness lurks beyond the margins of the mundane, emerging to dismantle our assumptions of reality. Dark in the Day is an anthology of weird fiction, penned by established writers and also those new to the genre – the latter being authors who are, or were, students of Creative Writing at Staffordshire University, where editor Storm Constantine occasionally delivers guest lectures. Her co-editor, Paul Houghton, is the senior lecturer in Creative Writing at the university.

Contributors include: Martina Bellovičová, J. E. Bryant, Glynis Charlton, Storm Constantine, Louise Coquio, Elizabeth Counihan, Krishan Coupland, Elizabeth Davidson, Siân Davies, Paul Finch, Rosie Garland, Rhys Hughes, Kerry Fender, Andrew Hook, Paul Houghton, Tanith Lee, Tim Pratt, Nicholas Royle, Michael Marshall Smith, Paula Wakefield, Ian Whates and Liz Williams.
ISBN: 978-1-907737-74-9 £11.99, $18.99

Blood, the Phoenix and a Rose by Storm Constantine

Wraeththu, a race of androgynous beings, have arisen from the ashes of human civilisation. Like the mythical rebis, the divine hermaphrodite, they represent the pinnacle of human evolution. But Wraeththu – or hara – were forged in the crucible of destruction and emerged from a new Dark Age. They have yet to realise their full potential and come to terms with the most blighted aspects of their past. Blood, the Phoenix and a Rose begins with an enigma: Gavensel, a har who appears unearthly and has a shrouded history. He has been hidden away in the house of Sallow Gandaloi by Melisander, an alchemist, but is this seclusion to protect Gavensel from the world or the world from him? As his story unfolds, the shadow of the dark fortress Fulminir falls over him, and memories of his past slowly return. The only way to find the truth is to go back through the layers of time, to when the blood was fresh. ISBN: 978-1-907737-75-6 £11.99, $18.99

Animate Objects by Tanith Lee

There is no such thing as an inanimate object… And how could that be? Because, simply, everything is formed from matter, and basically, at *root*, the matter that makes up everything in the physical world – the Universe – is of the same substance. Which means, on that basic level, we – you, me, and that power station over there – are all the exact riotous, chaotic, amorphous *same*. Here is an assortment of Lee takes on the nature, and perhaps intentions, of so-called non-sentient things. And you're quite safe. This is only a book. An inanimate object.

From the Introduction by Tanith Lee

The original hardback of this collection, of which there were only 35 copies, was published by Immanion Press in 2013, to commemorate Tanith Lee receiving the Lifetime Achievement Award at World Fantasycon. It included 5 previously unpublished pieces. This new release includes a further 2 stories, co-written by Tanith Lee and John Kaiine, and new interior illustrations by Jarod Mills. ISBN: 978-1-907737-73-2, £11.99 $18.99

Immanion Press
http://www.immanion-press.com
info@immanion-press.com

Lightning Source UK Ltd.
Milton Keynes UK
UKOW03f2333230517

301878UK00001B/135/P